I Don't Want a Rabbit

Ingrid Prins & Jelena Brezovec

Clavis

NEW YORK

"I want a new rabbit," Dad says.
"Me too," Mom says. "Shall we get a black one this time,
or one with white spots?"
I shake my head. I don't want a rabbit.

"Sure," Dad says. "A new rabbit to hold on your lap."
Mom nods.
I think of Blossom. Blossom wasn't just a rabbit to hold on your lap.
"Yes," Mom says. "Let's do it. I really want a new one."
"I don't," I say.
"I never want another rabbit."

The next morning a little brown rabbit is sitting on our doorstep.
Right in front of our door.
What's it doing here? I don't want it.
"Get away from our doorstep," I say.
The rabbit lifts one ear, but the other one is drooping.
Just like Blossom.
I close the door, right in the rabbit's face.

After a while I look out the window. The rabbit is still there.
He looks at me and washes his nose.
"You can't stay here," I say, but the rabbit doesn't move.

I try to lure him away.
"Hey, come over here!" I call.
"Look… I have something special for you."
The rabbit doesn't react.
"Don't you like carrots?" I add. "Come on."

Then I don't know
what to do.

I stand and yell:
"We don't like rabbits!"

I get the biggest pan lids I can find.
BING, BANG, BONG, CLASH, CLANG.

I make so much noise, I'll get rid of that rabbit.
The neighbors come out and hold their hands over their ears.
BING, BANG, BONG, CLASH, CLANG.

I keep going until I can't lift my arms anymore.

It worked! The doorstep is empty.
Relieved, I sit down.

clash
clang

bing bang

Then I hear a soft plop behind me.
And another one, a bit louder. I look around.

"Go away," I whisper.
The rabbit wiggles his whiskers and jumps towards me.
"Go away," I say.
He pushes his nose against my shoe.
"Stop it." I lean down to push him away.
He's so soft! And he smells like bunnies. Just like Blossom.
I quickly withdraw my hand.

"Buzz off!"
I yell at the brown bunny.
"I don't want
a rabbit!"

There, that's done.
This fence will keep him out.

Perfect.

Ding-dong!
The mailman has a package for us.
I open our door a crack,
but the wind is blowing too hard.
"Close the door!" Dad yells.

The rabbit jumps inside.
"You can't go back there!" I say.
He is looking at our living room.

"Not in the cage."

I make sure he can't get at it.

"Hey, that's my butt."
The rabbit wiggles his bottom.
"Yes," I say. "And that's yours."
The rabbit wiggles again.
I giggle. I can't help it.

"Dad?" I ask. My voice sounds a bit hoarse.
"Do you ever think about Blossom?"
"Of course I do," he says.
"Do you remember how sweet she was?"
"Very sweet," Dad answers.
"She was, wasn't she?" I say.
"Blossom was adorable," Dad says,
"I'll never forget Blossom."

Blossom was the sweetest bunny in the world.
One morning, she was lying still in her cage. Just like that.
Her tummy didn't move anymore.
I called for Mom and she saw it too.
At first I was afraid, but then I petted Blossom.
She was just as soft as before.
And sweet.
So sweet it made me cry.
Apart from that, she was mostly cold and silent.

"Mom!" I yell. "Come and look!"
"Aw, that's a sweet little bunny," she says.

He huddles against me.
I bury my nose in his fur.
That's nice. We stay that way for a long time.

"I like you," I whisper.
The rabbit starts and stands up.
"Don't get up," I say quickly.
He lies down again, even closer than before.
I put my hand on his head.
He lifts one ear and lets the other one droop.
I tickle the top of his head.
"Mom?" I ask. "Can this bunny stay with us?
He's almost as sweet as Blossom."

"The bunny sleeps with me tonight," I say. "I want him to stay."

"No," Mom says. "When you go to sleep, the rabbit goes in the cage."

"All night long?" I ask.

Mom nods.

"He can stay until Dad is done reading. Then he goes downstairs."

That means I have to go all night with no bunny. I sigh.

Dad grabs a book. "Don't read too fast," I say.

Then I dive under the covers until I'm an inch from the rabbit. I whisper:

"Tomorrow when I wake up, I'll come and see you right away."